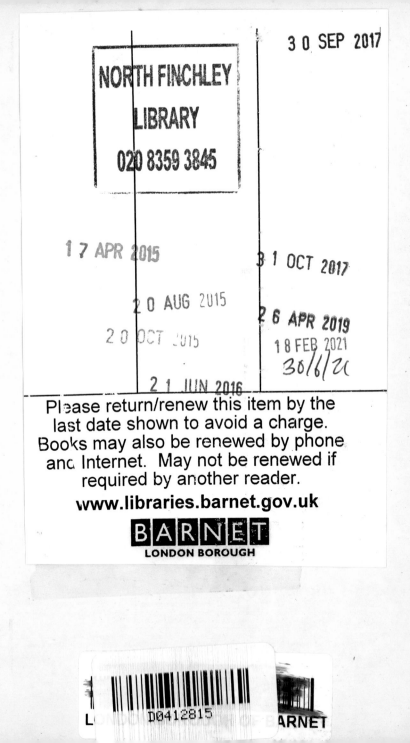

To Lara and Isla, two wonderful sisters

Special thanks to
Rachel Elliot

ORCHARD BOOKS
338 Euston Road, London NW1 3BH
Orchard Books Australia
Level 17/207 Kent Street, Sydney, NSW 2000
A Paperback Original

First published in 2015 by Orchard Books

A CIP catalogue record for this book is available
from the British Library.

ISBN 978 1 40833 938 1

1 3 5 7 9 10 8 6 4 2

Printed and bound by CPI Group (UK) Ltd, Croydon, CR0 4YY

MIX
Paper from
responsible sources
FSC® C104740
FSC
www.fsc.org

The paper and board used in this book are made from wood from responsible sources.

Orchard Books is an imprint of Hachette Children's Group
and published by The Watts Publishing Group Limited, an Hachette UK company.

www.hachette.co.uk

Frances
the Royal Family
Fairy

by Daisy Meadows

ORCHARD

www.rainbowmagic.co.uk

Jack Frost's
Ice Castle

The High St.

Kirsty's House

Jack Frost's Spell

Royal babies make me snore.
I've never been so bored before.
Their family's too dull to mention
It's time that I got some attention!

I'll make a sibling presently
Who'll be as bold and bad as me,
And think I'm handsome, brave and clever.
I'll be the coolest brother ever!

Contents

A New
Fairy Friend

Two magical invitations from Fairyland
were lying on Kirsty Tate's bed. As she
and her best friend Rachel Walker got
dressed, they both kept glancing at the
invitations. The delicate green leaves
glimmered with swirly golden writing:

Princess Grace and Prince Arthur are delighted to announce the birth of their second child. A beautiful sibling for Prince George!

You are invited to celebrate the new arrival and attend a welcoming ceremony at the Royal Fairyland Palace.

Someone special will collect you both at midday on Saturday!

"We are so lucky," said Rachel, pinning a sparkling flower clip into her hair. "This will be the second royal baby ceremony we've attended."

"I wonder if it will be like Prince George's ceremony," said Kirsty, remembering that special day.

"Hopefully Jack Frost has behaved himself this time!"

Before Prince George's naming ceremony, naughty Jack Frost and his mischievous goblins had stolen Georgie the Royal Prince Fairy's royal seal.

The girls smoothed down their frilly skirts and smiled at each other. They had been so happy when the invitations wafted through their bedroom windows

three days ago. It was always exciting
to get a message from their fairy friends,
but a royal ceremony was very special
indeed.

Kirsty brushed
her glossy hair
and then laid her
brush down on her
dressing table.

"Well, we're
ready," said Rachel,
looking at her watch.
"It's almost midday.
Who do you think is coming
to collect us? Will it be Georgie?"

"It could be anyone," said Kirsty,
thinking of all the fairies they had met.
"We're lucky to have shared so many
magical adventures with them."

"Perhaps it'll be a fairy you've never
met before," said a laughing voice.

They whirled around and saw
a beautiful fairy standing on the
windowsill, her wand raised in the air.
The light spring breeze swished her blue
silky dress, and her
long, dark hair was
set off with a
sparkling tiara.

"I'm Frances
the Royal
Family Fairy,"
she said.
"I'm here to
take you to
the ceremony.
You both look
wonderful!"

13

"You too," said Rachel with a big smile. "We're really looking forward to it! Are you going to be part of the ceremony?"

"Yes," Frances replied. "I have a magical rubber duck wearing a crown, which helps me to watch over royal siblings. I make sure that they play happily together, share their toys and have lots of fun."

"Lucky royal baby," said Kirsty. "I bet Prince George will be a wonderful big brother."

"Are you ready to go?" asked Frances. The girls nodded, and Frances flew above them, sprinkling fairy dust over their heads. At once they felt themselves shrinking to fairy size, and in a moment they were fluttering in front of Kirsty's

dressing-table mirror. Frances pointed her
wand at the mirror, and the glass began
to shimmer and ripple.

"Through the glass to Fairyland," she
said, with a tinkling laugh.

Hand in hand, Rachel and Kirsty
fluttered forward. Feeling a little unsure,
they reached out to touch the glass. Their
hands simply slid through it!

"Ooh, it tickles!" said Kirsty, giggling
as they flew forward.

15

As the best friends passed through
the glass, they closed their eyes. For a
moment their skin felt warm and tickly.
Then they opened their eyes and found
themselves stepping onto the lawn of the
Fairyland Palace.

Blinking in the Fairyland sunshine, the
girls heard a chorus of friendly voices
calling their names and greeting them.
A crowd of fairies was on the lawn,
chattering and playing with Prince
George and a rosy-cheeked fairy baby.
Rachel and Kirsty saw many of their
friends, including Georgie the Royal
Prince Fairy, Kate the Royal Wedding
Fairy, Alexandra the Royal Baby Fairy
and Jennifer the Babysitter Fairy.

Frances hurried forward and gave each
baby a hug.

"Hello, Prince George!" said Rachel.
Prince George waved a chubby hand
and put his arm around the baby.

"Wow, you're a really good big
brother," said Kirsty with a smile.

"He shares his toys really well," said
Georgie, fluttering over to hug them.

"And he's so kind," added Jennifer. "The new baby is very lucky."

As Rachel and Kirsty greeted and hugged their fairy friends, they heard a loud bonging sound. Bertram the frog footman was standing outside the palace, striking a large, bronze gong. His chest was puffed out and he looked very important.

"Their Royal Highnesses request that all honoured guests make their way to the Throne Room for the Royal Ceremony," he announced.

Rachel and Kirsty smiled at Bertram and followed the fairies into the palace, chattering about the ceremony. The

babies fluttered beside them, gurgling
with excitement. In the Throne Room,
the king and queen were standing beside
their thrones with Prince Arthur and
Princess Grace. Frances took her place
beside them, holding a rubber duck in
her hand. Rachel
smiled when she
noticed that it
was wearing
a golden
crown.
Prince
George
held the
baby's hand
and flew
towards the
beautiful crib.

19

The queen welcomed everyone and
then each group of fairies stepped
forward in turn to give a magical gift.
The Fun Day Fairies gave him the
gift of laughter, and the Sporty Fairies
gave him the gift of sporting skills. One
by one, the fairies presented wonderful
presents to the new arrival. All the way
through the ceremony, Prince George
held the baby's hand.

Everyone cheered
and clapped when
all the gifts had
been given. But
before the cheers
stopped, there
was a loud crash
of thunder and
Jack Frost appeared.

Frances cried out as he grabbed the
rubber duck out of her hands and then
vanished with a flash of blue lightning.
At that moment, Prince George shook off
the baby's hand and snatched the rattle.

The Royal Family Fairy's magic had
been stolen!

Too Many Ducks

"Prince George, give back that rattle," said his mother in a low voice.

Prince George shook his head and started to cry. Everyone looked shocked and upset, and Frances rushed over to the queen and whispered urgently in her ear.

Queen Titania nodded and then looked at Rachel and Kirsty.

"Girls, we're going to need your help," she said. "This is a very serious situation. Without Frances's rubber duck, royal siblings in the human and fairy worlds will be suffering, and this will affect their kingdoms."

"What can we do?" asked Kirsty at once.

"Will you go to the Ice Castle?" the queen asked. "Try to get the rubber duck back before too much damage is done."

"Of course we will," said Rachel.

"Take Frances with you," said Queen
Titania. "She has never been to the Ice
Castle before, but she will be able to
recognise her rubber duck."

Frances and the girls
flew out of the
Throne Room
and zoomed up
into the bright sky.
But for once the
sunshine didn't
make them smile
– they had to stop
Jack Frost from
spoiling everything.
If royal siblings
couldn't get on, they
could be too busy arguing to
run their kingdoms or make decisions.

They soon arrived at the grey and gloomy Ice Castle. A black cloud was hovering above it, and the three fairies fluttered up to hide behind it.

"What are those things on the battlements?" asked Kirsty, peering down.

There was a row of rubber ducks lined up all the way around the castle, looking outwards as if they were on guard duty.

"Jack Frost must have guessed that we'd come after him," said Rachel. "Has he hidden your rubber duck somewhere among all these?"

But Frances shook her head.

"Not a single one of them is wearing a crown," she said.

"Let's get closer," Kirsty suggested. "Maybe it's just out of sight. There don't seem to be any goblins on guard."

But as they swooped down towards the castle, several goblin guards jumped up from behind the battlements. They picked up the rubber ducks and started throwing them at the fairies.

"Ha ha, you'll never find Jack Frost so you might as well give up!" cackled one.

"Push off, silly fairies!" crowed another.

"Fly back!" cried Kirsty, dodging sideways to avoid another duck.

They darted out of throwing range, and then Frances let out a loud exclamation.

"There he is!" she called out. "There's Jack Frost!"

She pointed towards the forest beside the castle, but Rachel and Kirsty could only see snow-covered branches, shivering in the icy wind.

"Where?" they asked, as the goblins continued to hurl rubber ducks at them.

"He disappeared into the forest," said Frances. "Come on, let's catch up with him!"

The fairies zoomed into the forest. It was dark and cold, and the only sound they could hear was the wind whistling through the trees.

"Where is he?" asked Rachel in a whisper. "Can you see him?"

The others shook their heads. They flew forwards slowly, peering into the shadows. Strange shapes loomed out of the darkness, becoming crooked branches, tree stumps and large bushes as they fluttered closer.

"We'll never find him in here," said Frances with a groan. "We've lost him."

They stopped beside a large holly bush.

"Shall we fly up and see if we can spot him from above?" Kirsty suggested.

Suddenly they heard a shriek of fury, and then Jack Frost sprang up behind the holly bush!

"I knew there was someone following me!" he raged. "What are you doing in MY forest?"

"Don't let him see we're scared," said Rachel in a low voice.

"Give back Frances's rubber duck," said Kirsty. "It's wrong to take things that belong to other people."

"It's mine now," snapped Jack Frost. "So

it's none of your business!"

"Why do you want the rubber duck?" Frances asked. "It's no use to you."

"I'm fed up of all the talk about royal fairy siblings," Jack Frost said. "It's gone on long enough. It's time that everyone started talking about ME and MY sibling."

"But you don't have a sibling," said Rachel, puzzled. "You created a twin for yourself once and you didn't like him!"

"Jimmy Thaw was too nice," said Jack Frost with a sneer. "This time I can magic up something MUCH better, thanks to the rubber ducky."

"You mustn't!" Frances exclaimed.

"Mustn't?" repeated Jack Frost, raising his eyebrows. "Nobody says 'mustn't' to me!"

A New Sibling

Rachel tried to argue, but her words were drowned out by a deafening crash as Jack Frost aimed a thunderbolt at them. Suddenly the sky was raining rubber ducks and they dived for cover.

"Stop it!" cried Kirsty.

"He's gone!" Rachel called out.

The rubber ducks stopped falling and the three fairies stared at each other in alarm.

"This is even worse than I thought," said Frances. "He's going to use my magical rubber duck  to make a sibling just like himself."

"We have to keep searching," said Kirsty. "We have to stop him before he creates a second Jack Frost!"

The fairies sped through the shadowy forest, but however hard they looked, they couldn't spot Jack Frost. All they saw were hundreds and hundreds of rubber ducks, in all colours and styles. The ducks were lined up on tree branches, balancing on bushes and peeking out from among the flowers.

"This is hopeless," said Frances with a groan. "I feel as if we've flown around the forest three times already. I'm sure I've seen that blue duck over there before."

Just then, Kirsty spotted a flash of blue light through a gap between two fir trees.

"What was that?" she asked.

"Let's find out," said Rachel, zooming forward.

When they arrived at the clearing, they stopped and stared in shock. Jack Frost was holding Frances's magical rubber duck up in the air, surrounded by swirling icicles and crackles of blue lightning.

"Rubber ducky, make me lucky!
Create a sibling mean and yucky.
Someone who will share my dreams,
And help with all my tricks and schemes!"

"Stop!" cried Frances.

Jack Frost saw her, but he just grinned and held the rubber duck even higher.

"Too late!" he shrieked.

There was a rumble of thunder, a bright-blue flash, and then a second figure appeared next to Jack Frost. The fairies gasped. She had the same sharp nose and spiky hair, the same narrow eyes and sour expression. When she saw the fairies, she gave a very unpleasant grin.

"My big brother's too clever for you," she sneered. "I'm Jilly Chilly, and you are going to give me my first bit of fun."

37

Before they could reply, Jilly Chilly raised her wand. Ropes appeared from nowhere and snaked around the fairies as fast as lightning, pinning their wings and arms down by their sides. Frances's wand dropped from her hand onto a pile of leaves.

"Ha ha!" Jack Frost said, hooting with laughter. "That's the funniest thing I've seen all day!"

Jilly Chilly linked arms with him and they stalked off together, cackling with laughter.
As their flowing cloaks disappeared from sight, Rachel, Kirsty and Frances exchanged worried looks. They were trapped!

"The light's fading," said Frances, looking up and shivering. "It'll be dark soon and we're only wearing thin dresses. We have to think of a way to get free!"

Kirsty was still gazing after Jack Frost and Jilly Chilly. As she peered into the gloomy shadows, she thought she saw a pair of eyes watching her.

"I think there's someone over there," she said, nodding her head in that direction. "Yes, there is! I just saw them blink."

"Who could it be?" asked Frances, sounding a bit scared.

But Rachel had an idea.

"Don't worry," she said in a confident voice. "I expect it's one of the animals of the forest. They might even be able to help us."

"Good thinking!" said Kirsty. "All animals love fairies!"

"Animals of the forest!" called Frances in a loud voice. "If you're listening, we really need your help. Jack Frost and his sister have captured us and tied us up. We have to get free and stop their nasty plans, or fairy and human royal families will suffer."

"Please help us," added Kirsty, looking at the trees all around them. "If you're on the side of the fairies and the royal family, come and help us to get free."

Cleaning
the Castle

The fairies waited. For a moment all they
could hear was the rustling of the leaves
in the breeze. Then there was a scurrying,
shuffling sound that got louder and
louder. Squirrels, mice, moles and rabbits
crept out into the clearing and came
shyly towards the fairies. One by one
they started to nibble at the ropes. It took

a long time, but at last the ropes began to come loose.

"Yes!" Rachel exclaimed as her bonds fell away.

She rubbed her arms where the rope had been so tight. Kirsty and Frances were soon free too, and Frances picked up her wand.

"Before we do anything else, we need warm clothes," she said.

She swished her wand and instantly the three of them were snuggling into thick, furry capes with pixie hoods.

"Now we have to follow Jack Frost and get the rubber duck back," said Kirsty.

"Before he and Jilly Chilly cause any more trouble," Rachel added.

They flew up through the snow-covered trees. It was evening now, and there were no stars because it was too cloudy. But in the distance, they could see lights shining out of the darkness.

"That's the Ice Castle," said Kirsty. "I've never seen it so lit up before."

They zoomed towards it, and a few minutes later they were hovering outside the window of the Throne Room.

To their surprise, they could see goblins hard at work inside, all wearing aprons and rubber gloves. Some were hanging flowery blue wallpaper while others lay a thick blue carpet on the floor. Others were scrubbing the cobwebs and dust from walls and high corners.

"How odd," said Rachel. "I've never seen the goblins working so hard before."

"The windows are sparkling," said Frances. "It looks as if they've just been polished."

"The goblins look scared," Kirsty added. "They're not even complaining!"

"Something strange is going on in the castle," said Rachel with a frown. "Frances, could you disguise us as goblins? Then we can find out what's happening."

One of the windows was open a crack, and the three fairies slipped inside and hid behind a billowing, flowery curtain. Frances waved her wand, and instantly the girls' wings disappeared. Their noses grew and their skin turned a sickly shade of green.

47

"Oh dear, we look awful!" said Kirsty with a squawky goblin giggle.

"Are you sure this is a good idea?" asked Frances, looking nervous. "What if they realise that you're in disguise?"

"Don't worry about us," said Rachel, smiling at the little fairy. "We've had lots of practice at pretending to be goblins!"

She and Kirsty each took a deep breath and then stepped out from behind the curtain.

"You're late!" snapped a bad-tempered voice. "Why aren't you wearing your aprons and rubber gloves?"

A spindly, pimply goblin was glaring at Rachel and Kirsty with his hands on his hips.

"Why should we?" said Rachel, trying to sound like a normal, rude goblin.

"Because Jilly Chilly said so," said the spindly goblin. "And you don't want to get on the wrong side of her, believe me. There are three goblins cleaning the toilets with toothbrushes because they answered back to her."

"We saw her earlier," said Kirsty. "Jack Frost seemed to like her."

"He thinks she's wonderful," said the goblin in a gloomy voice. "He's letting her do whatever she wants — starting with cleaning and redecorating the castle."

"She's awful," said a short goblin with a wobbly belly. "All she does is shout at us and take bubble baths with that stupid rubber ducky."

"She's almost used up all the water in the castle with her baths and her silly cleaning," said the spindly goblin.

Rachel and Kirsty exchanged excited glances. It sounded as if Jilly Chilly had the rubber duck. They had to find her!

A Chilly Bath

"It seems as if we'd be better off without Jack Frost's new sister," said Rachel.

"She doesn't like us at all," said a third goblin, whose nose was dripping. "We're not special to Jack Frost any more because he listens to everything she says. I think she's going to get rid of us!"

"I know how we can stop him liking her so much," said Kirsty, thinking fast. "Without the rubber duck, the sibling magic he used to create her will be very weak."

"We should steal it!" cried the short goblin at once.

"Hide it!" exclaimed the spindly goblin.

"Eat it!" shouted the goblin with the drippy nose.

The short goblin gave him a shove.

"Don't be an idiot," he snapped. "You can't eat a rubber ducky!"

The drippy goblin shoved him back, and the

girls could see that a typical goblin fight was about to break out.

"I think hiding it is the best idea," said Rachel in a firm voice. "We'll do it – she hasn't seen us before."

None of the goblins argued. Nobody wanted to go anywhere near Jilly Chilly if they could help it! Just then, a terrible shriek echoed through the castle.

"I want more bubbles for my bath now," screeched Jilly Chilly's voice. "And I mean NOW!"

Kirsty glanced over her shoulder to the curtains, where she knew Frances was hiding. She put her hands behind her back.

"Luckily, I've got some amazing new bubble bath," she said in a loud voice, hoping that Frances would take the hint.

Instantly, a large bottle of bubble bath appeared in her hands. She showed it to the other goblins.

"We'll take this to Jilly Chilly now," said Rachel. "Then we'll take the rubber duck while she's trying out the new bubbles."

"Good idea," said the short goblin. "But don't expect me to help you."

"Yeah, she'll make you clean the dungeons with a wet fish if she catches you," added the spindly goblin with a snigger.

For once, Rachel and Kirsty felt glad that the goblins were so selfish. They didn't want anyone coming with them to take the rubber duck! Soon they were hurrying along the surprisingly clean corridors, following the sound of splashing water and Jilly Chilly's screeching voice.

"I hope that Frances waits for us in the Throne Room," said Kirsty as they ran.

"She will," said Rachel. "I'm sure she heard our plan."

"Do you think this is going to work?" asked Kirsty, feeling a bit worried.

Rachel was nervous too, but she smiled to make her best friend feel better.

"Of course it is," she said.

They arrived at the bathroom and pushed open the door. The floor was covered with water and wet towels lay all around. In the centre of the room was a large bath with claw feet, and Jilly Chilly was sitting in it. Her fists were clenched and she was thumping the edge of the bath and kicking her legs in fury. Icy

water splashed over the girls and they
squealed.

"You two ugly nincompoops had better
have some bubbles for me!" she screamed.

Rachel held up the bottle and Jilly
Chilly stopped splashing. The girls poured
the bubbles into the bath and added
more water, but they only had eyes for
one thing. Bobbing around Jilly Chilly
was a little rubber duck wearing a
golden crown.

"Can you reach it?" Rachel mouthed
to Kirsty behind Jilly Chilly's back.

Kirsty tried, but as she reached out her
hand Jilly Chilly turned around. She was
just too close to the duck for them to be
able to take it. What could they do?

"I want to make waves," said Jilly
Chilly.

"You shouldn't make waves in the bath," said Kirsty, forgetting that she was supposed to be a goblin. "It's naughty."

"Quiet!" said Jilly Chilly with a scowl. "Watch this!"

She started to slide backwards and forwards in the bath, swooshing the water. She shrieked with laughter as the waves grew higher…and higher… and higher! Water splashed across the floor and bubbles landed on everything

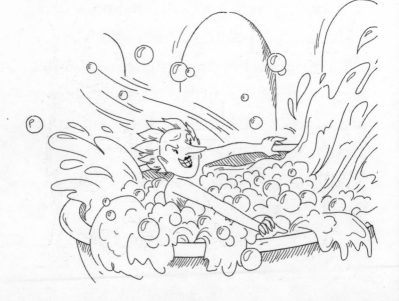

– including Rachel and Kirsty. But they were watching the little rubber duck. It was surfing the very top of a large wave.

"I think this might be our chance," said Rachel.

At that moment, the duck flew up into the air. Quick as a flash, Kirsty reached out her hand and caught it.

"Let's go!" she called to Rachel.

Still disguised as goblins, the girls pelted along the corridor, their hearts hammering. They were halfway to the Throne Room when they heard Jilly Chilly shriek.

"Where's my rubber ducky?" she screamed. "Get those goblins! I'll have them polishing the battlements with their bare hands! BRING IT BACK!"

Jack Frost Changes His Mind

"Faster!" said Rachel, panting as she sprinted towards the Throne Room. "Faster!"

They could hear the slap of wet feet pounding after them. The castle walls rang with Jilly Chilly's shrieks. At last they saw the Throne Room up ahead.

Kirsty put on an extra spurt of speed and burst through the door, where the other goblins were waiting for them.

"We got it!" Kirsty yelled.

The goblins cheered and reached out their hands to take it, but out of the corner of her eye, Kirsty saw Frances dart out of the window into the night, beckoning. Kirsty hurled the rubber duck through the window after the little fairy, and then stopped, gasping for breath. Rachel was close behind her.

"We did it!" she said.

None of the goblins heard her, because Jilly Chilly's wails were deafening. Suddenly the Throne Room door flew open again, and Jack Frost sprang into the room. His face was lined with frowns.

"Who's making that terrible racket?" he demanded, curling his lip.

"JILLY CHILLY!" shouted all the goblins together – even Rachel and Kirsty.

"Well I can't live with someone who makes that sort of noise!" he thundered. "Where is she? I'm going to reverse that spell right now and send her back where she came from. One of you lot should have told me the truth; little sisters are really ANNOYING!"

As soon as the door banged shut behind him, the goblins tore off their aprons and flung their gloves into the air, cheering and dancing around arm in arm.

Unnoticed, Rachel and Kirsty slipped
over to the window and peered out.
Frances was hovering outside, holding her
rubber duck in her hand.

"Well done, both of you!" she
exclaimed happily. "Let's get out of here."

With a wave of her wand, Rachel and
Kirsty became fairies once again. The
goblins were so busy
leaping around the
Throne Room
and celebrating
that they
didn't see a
thing. The girls
fluttered out to
join Frances, and
they all shared a big
hug.

"Let's get back to the palace," said Frances. "I can't wait to see the Royal Family!"

As they zoomed and swooped away from the Ice Castle, the sky became clearer and the stars and moon appeared. Soon they saw the beautiful Fairyland Palace ahead of them, shining in the moonlight. They flew down and made their way to the Throne Room.

The king and queen were talking quietly, and the royal babies were playing happily together. They were obviously the best of friends again. When the guests saw Frances, Rachel and Kirsty, they started to applaud. Princess Grace came hurrying towards the girls, holding out her hands.

"Thank you from the bottom of

my heart," she said. "I knew you had succeeded as soon as the babies started to smile at each other again."

"Our family is happy again," added Prince Arthur, "and royal families across the human world are safe too – thanks to you."

Rachel and Kirsty curtseyed, and then shared another hug with Frances.

"You've been wonderful," she said.

"I wouldn't have been able to save my rubber duck or make the royal babies be friends without you."

"You're welcome," said Kirsty and Rachel together.

It was time for them to go home. Frances swished her wand in front of them, and everything started to shimmer. A few moments later they were standing in front of Kirsty's mirror, and the sun was shining through the window. Their cosy capes had disappeared.

"I'm so pleased that royal families are all happy again," said Rachel. "Isn't it great that we were able to help?"

Kirsty nodded, thinking of all the smiling faces at the ceremony. Just then, her bedroom door opened and Mrs Tate looked in.

"Oh, what lovely dresses!" she exclaimed. "Are you playing a dressing-up game? What fun! I just wanted to tell you that fairy cakes and lemonade are waiting for you downstairs, when you're ready."

She left, and the girls smiled at each other. Mrs Tate didn't know that it was much more than a game.

"I'm so happy that we have such amazing adventures in Fairyland," said Rachel, hugging her best friend.

"Me too," said Kirsty. "And I'm so happy that I have you to share them with!"

Now it's time for Kirsty and Rachel to help...

Daisy the Festival Fairy

Read on for a sneak peek...

"Get ready for a bumpy ride!" said Mr Walker.

Rachel Walker and her best friend Kirsty Tate giggled as the car drove through an uneven field. They were both fizzing with excitement.

"I can't believe we really have tickets for the Rainbow Days Festival!" said Rachel. "I keep thinking I must be dreaming."

The festival was so popular that tickets sold out very quickly. The Walkers had always wanted to go, but this was the first time they had been successful.

"What are you looking forward to most, girls?" asked Mrs Walker, turning to smile at them.

"Dressing up!" said Rachel at once. "I love the way that each day has a colourful theme – today is a circus theme, Saturday is carnival and Sunday is 80s fashion."

"I can't wait for the music concerts each day," said Kirsty. "Lots of our favourite groups are going to be here, like the Angels and Groove Gang and Jacob Bright."

"But hopefully *not* the Gobolicious Band," said Rachel in a quiet voice.

Kirsty grinned and crossed her fingers. They were the only humans who knew that Frosty and his Gobolicious Band were Jack Frost and his goblins in disguise. Jack Frost was always trying to make trouble for the fairies, and Rachel and Kirsty had often helped their fairy friends to foil his plans.

"Look!" said Kirsty, as the car bounced over a particularly large bump. "There's the family camping area."

She pointed to a grassy space full of tents, which was surrounded by a circle of silver birch trees. Someone had painted a large sign on a piece of driftwood:

Welcome to the
Silver Birch Family Campsite

Mr Walker parked the car next to a small tepee with the number 11 painted on the side. Then he turned to look at the girls.

"Surprise!" he said. "We're going to sleep in our ordinary tent, but we've hired a tepee for you girls as a special treat."

Rachel undid her seatbelt and flung her arms around her dad's neck.

"That's amazing, thank you!" she exclaimed.

"Thank you, Mr and Mrs Walker!" Kirsty added. "This weekend just gets better and better!"

The best friends jumped out of the car and pulled their bags out of the boot.

"Let's go and unpack," said Rachel. "I can't wait to see what it's like!"

They ducked their heads to go inside, and both said, "Ooh!" at the same time. The tepee was filled with velvety throws, cushions and sheepskins. Two thick mattresses lay on the floor, and a rainbow spiral mobile hung from the top. The floor was covered with a thick woven rug.

"I love it!" said Rachel, running inside

and twirling around with her arms outstretched. "I wish I could sleep in one all the time!"

There was a list of events pinned to the wall of the tepee. Rachel and Kirsty quickly unpacked their things and then sat down to look at the list.

"Shall we go and look around right now?" said Kirsty.

Rachel popped her head out of the tepee and saw her parents setting up their tent.

"Is it OK if we go and explore?" she called.

"Of course," said Mrs Walker. "We'll meet you back here at lunchtime, OK?"

Rachel agreed, and she and Kirsty quickly pulled on their colourful circus outfits. Rachel had a glittery purple waistcoat with a stripy skirt, and Kirsty chose a dress covered with multi-coloured spots. Then they raced towards the main festival area.

Read **Daisy the Festival Fairy** to find out what adventures are in store for Kirsty and Rachel!

RAINBOW magic ®

Join in the magic online by signing up
to the Rainbow Magic fan club!

Meet the fairies, play games and
get sneak peeks at the latest books!

There's fairy fun for everyone at

www.rainbowmagicbooks.co.uk

You'll find great activities, competitions, stories and
fairy profiles, and also a special newsletter.

Find a fairy with
your name!